A VISIT TO LIFE

24 Flashes

— Conrad Bishop —

Edited by Elizabeth Fuller

WordWorkers Press
Sebastopol CA

A VISIT TO LIFE: 24 Flashes
© 2023 Conrad Bishop

Printed in the United States of America.

For information:
indepeye@gmail.com

For purchases:
www.damnedfool.com

ISBN: 979-8-9856835-3-0

Contents

Foreword

As human, we search vehemently for ultimate meaning. Perhaps because we know we're going to die, we put faith in religions, political movements, parenting, or baseball pennant races that promise a purpose to it all. Even those who maintain its pointlessness—that vast struggle of our molecules to stay glued together—write long books on the absence of meaning.

It's natural, then, that in picking up even this slender volume, there's an expectation of ultimate intention. What does the author want to express? And of course there's intention. If you get out of bed in the morning you can't avoid it. Whether your role is postal clerk, mother, or state executioner, you intend at least to get through the day and eat supper, if you can find it.

But intention may not signal intention. A mirror is fabricated with the aim of allowing us to check our hairs, but the mirror itself has no such intention. It just does its mirror thing. Same with this writer. Somewhere in there are many intentions—to survive, to be loved, to grab some moments of pleasure—but that's just the way I've been shaped. If the Great Beyond intended to shape me into a writer with only an unconscious purpose, well, that's what it did.

I recall our first trip to Europe, summer 1969. We traveled three months on a decrepit motor scooter, camping, eating meals out of a tin pot, over England, Ireland, France, Spain, Italy, Germany and the Netherlands. Some days were heaven, others were hell. Some days we learned survival skills; others we depended on the kindness of strangers.

So these pieces don't reflect a consistent point of view, or if they do, the POV is vastly diverse. Life is horrible, life is sweet. Life is stark nuts, life is just what it is. Life is definitely worth a visit. ∎

Big Lake

This is a tale of desire: desire at age eleven. At age eighty, it's still part of my lifeblood.

Desire meaning ambition, aspiration, lust—all those virtues that produce billionaires, astronauts, despots, explorers bringing disease and Coca-Cola—a desire for stupendous achievement. Such was my hike to Big Lake.

Big Lake is a big lake under clay bluffs to the north of Council Bluffs, Iowa. The bluffs gave the name to the town. There was a council between the Pottawatomies and the whiteskins, where the Pottawatomies neglected the needfui task of killing all the whiteskins. The lake was still there, the Pottawatomies were long gone.

I was the only child of a single mom, an ordinary kid with a bike and baseball cards. I got all A's but concealed the gaffe from my friends. I wasn't good at sports, but not bad—when I came to bat nobody made vomit sounds, as with James. When I was a Cub Scout, I earned lots of badges. My mom was very proud.

At eleven, you graduate to Boy Scouts. Troop Nine met in the basement of a church. First night, I went in and there were all these big kids, twelve to fourteen, and they all knew stuff that I didn't know. I didn't know what it was I didn't know, but I knew that they knew it.

I was put in the Panther Patrol, which was the best patrol, according to them, a gung-ho attitude, kinda *We'll tie knots in anything!* I was thrilled to be in the Panther Patrol.

With a problem. They were going on a Saturday bicycle hike to Big Lake, and I could go along. But my mom would say no. I knew it. I knew every word.

Not that she was over-protective. I took care of myself from age five, since the only baby-sitter on tap was a drunk. And I'd go off for hours on my bike to neighborhoods far away. But a hike with older boys around a lake—that didn't set right. So we went at it.

We fought on Wednesday, we fought on Thursday, we fought on Friday. "You're not going out there, you don't know those kids, what if you get lost, what if it rains, what if you run into hoboes? You got your whole life." On and on, and every point I dispelled with thunderous logic, but as Grandpa said, it was just tall cow pissing on flat rock.

My mother had the tenacity of a fireplug. No rhetoric would penetrate her will. But I discovered a weakness. You're on a freeway and you need to cut over. You signal, but the car to your right won't let you in. You try to go faster and they go faster, but then ... you give up and slow down. Amazing: they hang back and let you in. It almost never fails. Stick your paws in the air, whine *You win!* and suddenly, "Okay, that's cool, go ahead." The tactic is pretending to lose. Women are better at this, as they've had more practice, but I learned the secret early.

I gave up. I was the saddest, most pathetic little brat alive, and she couldn't stand it. "Okay, if it's good weather, if it's not going to rain, what time you have to get up? We'll see." So I pumped up my bike tires, got my pack ready, lunch packed, and even though they predicted rain, it couldn't rain. I was coming into my manhood.π

Saturday morning, it rained. Not hard, just a mist, those big drops were from tree leaves, and— My mother didn't pursue it. She'd worry herself to death, but that was her problem. My destiny was the Panther Patrol.

So I rode off and we met at the church, seven, eight kids, and set out to Big Lake, two, three miles to the north. A little rain, but it felt so good to be out early morning, seeing the sun peep through the clouds and a world washed clear. Eleven years old with guys who'd chosen me to be in the Panther Patrol.

We got to the parking area, and the idea was ride clear around on the trail to the top of the lake. Vernon said once they'd snuck up and seen a guy and a girl doing it. I had only a vague idea what you did if you were *doing it*, but it seemed like doing it was terrible and very exciting.

We started along the trail. The lake was all reeds and swamp, and then you'd hit big roots or face a gulch, so we were on our bikes and off, but we focused on the distant shore and its promise.

Then it rained.

Real rain. Insistent rain. Harder, like the bully pushing his thumb in your bicep, *Feel that?* Then harder: *Feel that!* We were wet, then soaked. We stopped under trees, then pushed our bikes into the torrent. I had a raincoat, but it was like swimming in a river, and the mud—

We forged on toward the top of the lake. And then we came to a stop. I realized, no, actually, I've got my whole life to see the guy and girl doing it, and in this weather, they're probably not doing it. The Panther Patrol turned like a flight of ducks and flew back with a mighty quack.

Or more like a trudge. The bluffs were clay, and the mud wasn't mud, it was super-glue. I'm lifting my bike through it, it clings to the tires, I scrape it out so the wheels can turn, then three yards on and they jam again. Then I'm carrying the bike, slipping down the banks, scrambling up, wearing great gobs of mud at the ends of my legs, lurching on. It felt like hours. Maybe half a mile back to the parking lot and that glorious span of asphalt.

I can't think how I got home. Just rode back, I guess. My mother, I don't think she did an *I-told-you-so*. She wasn't big on guilt.

But of course it's not ended, since now I'm recalling it. I'm still on that bike hike, still want to get there. Sure, now I know what that guy and that girl are doing, but I want to know what they're saying, their dreams, and then what happens through the rest of their lives. Did they get caught in the rain? Did they get through the mud okay? What're their names? ▪

Matchbooks

No school today, I'm home alone and Mom's at work. Mom has to work. She keeps their books, handles payroll, and drives a truck full of dynamite when they need it. She took me there once where she works, the sign says *Pitzer Construction*, a tin-roof shack down a gravel drive, two rooms, with desks for her and two old farts (what she calls them).

I don't know why I started the walk, maybe from just the desire or thinking to surprise her or from hating the empty rooms of the house, but I start the walk.

It's easy. Go south past the jog, turn the first road on the left, down the gravel, walk in, "It's you!" and maybe she'll come home early before my stepdad gets home. I don't like Lester, never did. He tries to be a dad.

I walk from our house down Silver Street, way far, then turn on the street just past where I go to the Saturday morning westerns with a Wild Bill Hickok serial, Episode 23 last week, and they threw him off the cliff. The road runs along a smelly stagnant ditch.

I won't know what to do when I get there, but I'm not getting there. I must have missed the turn. I can't find it, the turnoff, the street where my mother is, and I can't find the gravel drive. I'm lost in Rapid City, South Dakota, and Rapid City is cold.

It's freezing cold. I forgot my gloves, so I stick my hands in the pockets of my jeans, but the cold comes through. It's like the story the teacher read where the pioneers are freezing to death, but then they cut open a cow and get in, but I don't have a cow. If my hands froze stiff and I had no hands like the girl in the story who has no hands—

But I start to find paper matchbook covers along the road, and I stuff them into my pockets to keep out the cold.

People smoke and throw their matchbooks out the car windows for me to stuff in my pockets against the cold. It must have been a mile or more, but they keep my hands warm. They save my hands. The girl in the story does okay: she marries the king. But I'm not a girl and kings are only in stories. Maybe then they didn't have matchbooks. Maybe then they didn't smoke.

I get home and I find the key, but my hands are so cold I can barely fumble it. But I get the door open and then empty the matchbooks out of my pockets into my underwear drawer, maybe a dozen or so, and thank them for saving my hands. And I know that next Saturday, Wild Bill will be saved. Maybe he'll land in a tree.

~

A month or so later, my mom and my stepdad split up and we moved, so the matchbooks went into the trash. I felt bad to trash them, but they were old and smelly like Ragsie, our cocker spaniel, when she died.

And I knew that my mother would always come home from work without my having to find her. That was one thing I knew. And yes, Wild Bill fell into a tree, and the story went on. We survived. ∎

Marge

Margaret always hated to be called Marge. She'd warn her brothers, and once she smeared chickenshit on Franklin's hot dog, but it didn't do much good. She'd trained her husband Leroy out of it by giving him the stink eye three days in a row. But once you're a bookkeeper for a trucking company, you'd better get used to being called Marge.

Still, Hank called her Marge and she didn't mind.

Marge didn't have much to brag about for her sixty-odd years on Earth. Except that she'd survived as a single mom and raised a good son—a real achievement these days, like hitting the jackpot in Vegas. Even when they'd fought, she and her son Leroy Jr., it pleased her that he was as bull-headed as she was. Except once she'd seen him in a high school play where he died. His character died. She had to close her eyes. She heard his last line, and it sat there.

She'd lived for him, but now he had a family of his own, she saw him and the grandkids at Christmas and a week in the summer, and she didn't want to be intrusive. So she needed to make a life.

One thing she liked about Hank, who was Henry but went by Hank, on the first date he called her by name: Margaret. She liked him despite all else. He was a farmer, strike one: She'd grown up on a farm, couldn't stand farmers or farms. Strike two, he had an extended family and two old lobster sisters. From long experience she knew that it's family does you dirt. And he was Catholic. All those sacraments—two were enough for anyone—and the christalmighty Pope.

But Hank was a good dancer and had a sense of humor, which was better than that sonofabitch Lester. Two tries at husbands: Leroy, whom she loved but who ran off when the baby was born, and Lester, who died of a well-deserved heart attack. So she wasn't looking for marriage.

When Hank started talking the subject, she was cool at first, but she'd started thinking about old age and what she might leave to her son, and she started to come around. Hank had his own bank account, wouldn't dip into hers. She liked him okay, and he made her laugh. She said flat no to a Catholic wedding, but they might just go down to the county clerk.

He'd be picking her up at seven tonight to go to the dance in Omaha, and the question had to get settled. They had good times. They'd traveled down to the Ozarks to-gether, enjoyed the country shows, and he wasn't pushy. The sex thing wasn't big with her, but she could put up with it. The laughs were way better than sex.

His plan was to build their own house in the little town near the farm—he'd pay for that—and as soon as he could get out from under the farming, they'd sell the house and move to Omaha, where she had friends. It sounded okay. And she could put up with his Catholic stuff: she'd had a whole life of bullshit.

She'd asked her son what he thought. "Totally up to you, Mom, but a farmer will never leave the farm." She knew that her son was right. She could almost predict what would happen. They'd build their house—for him the first time off the farm in his own home, his sisters would hang on, so no way would he ever move, and she hated the little farm town. So they'd fight like cats and dogs when they were stuck at home, lovebirds when they went on vacation to the Ozarks or Las Vegas. Till one of them died and left the other with words unspoken.

There was Hank at the door. Knock knock. They all knock at the door. Leroy knocked, and she opened all the way. Lester knocked, and she opened just enough to have a sour eight months with him. Now Henry came knocking. Here goes. ▪

Maggie

He never talked to us much, to his daughters. Maybe his talking was all to Mom. He'd come back from a work trip, maybe gone six months, comes in the door, not a word, quick hug, "How's it going?" Then he'd go out drinking with Mom. We'd look at each other: *Oh, I guess that was Dad.*

But Mom said he was a good provider. "You need a man that puts food on the table. If he don't talk, that's okay, means you don't have to listen."

But when Mom was in the hospital, he wasn't a lot at the hospital or the house. "Nothing I can do for her there," he'd say. I think he hung out at the bar, maybe, tried for a pick-up. That week, he was just back from a job in Alaska, and my sisters were off somewhere, so I made supper and he talked. One blue streak. All through the two of us eating the meal. All through my doing the dishes. All through my not listening, although yes, I was.

He wasn't talking to me. Maybe to the wall. Maybe to Mom, as if she was sitting beside him on the bar stool. Maybe to his first wife that he left when he took up with Mom. Maybe to God or some other judge where he couldn't shut up. He never once looked at me.

~

So I was in a bar in Fairbanks, we were talking dogs, and I had a dog name of Maggie. Half husky, half wolf. And these guys, they're saying she's not half wolf, well she is, well she ain't. So I'm three sheets to the wind and—

Yeh, Fairbanks. And these were pretty rough guys, but I'm trying to get some money together so your mom wouldn't think I was such a sonofabitch— No, I mean that wasn't your mother then— That was before, that was Luann— But I'm talking about Maggie, my dog Maggie— Funny name, Maggie— So I say to these guys, "A hundred bucks she's a wolf!"

So we had a match, out back of the bar, dog on dog. And Maggie tore up about three of their dogs, I mean destroyed'em. And these guys were not happy. Dogs didn't come cheap, dogs like that, and here I'm making good money in construction, Aramco, biggest fucking oil company, pardon my French, while these guys, Navy Rescue, they're making about a quarter my salary. They go out picking guys off glaciers, talk about cold and nakedness, says in the Bible…

So here I am with a pile of bucks… Course I was three sheets to the wind…

~

"Do I want to hear this, Dad?" He didn't look like I'd said a word. Or even know who I was. I went back to doing the dishes.

~

So I'm walking back to the trailer, round the corner, and Maggie snarls. Here's ten guys, couple handguns. I grab onto Maggie, "Maggie, no!" And they lead us on down to a shed. Twelve huskies in there, no bets, eye for an eye, they just want that dog ripped. Certain point, you don't care about your pile of bucks, you just want blood. So in she goes, they slam the door—

You can't understand it, May—my name is April, my sister is May, he's got a bottle somewhere—the way people act when they're cold, they're alone, nobody gives a shit. No, sorry… But I hope you never… It's just…

— 11 —

And there were times, if I could live 'em over, I'd get some drinks in me— Go home to your mother, not your mother, no, but Luann, and— Okay if she'd yell at me, that was okay, but she'd freeze up and I just— I hit her—

And once she— May, you don't understand what I'm saying— She wouldn't do what you … do in a marriage, and I grabbed her and I did it anyway…

What was I…? So I look through a crack in the door, and Maggie disappears. Pack's on her like a blizzard. And chrissake I'm crying, it's a fucking dog—sorry—but she's all I got and I'm crying. And then—

The huskies start flying, rolling off, throats ripped, guts hanging out. Maggie's rolled on her back and she rips. That's how a wolf does, rolls on its back. They keep on coming, she keeps ripping. They don't know what's hit 'em. She killed five, four got away, two had to be shot. Most … satisfying moment of my life.

Course when I come back to the lower forty-eight, I couldn't keep her. I had to put her down.

~

Parents. Some, you love because you see them all the time, others you can't hardly stand except when they're gone. He acted as if he didn't quite know where he was or who he'd been talking to, but that was the booze, of course. Maybe he'd intended to tell the funny story, which he'd told a dozen times, about the rotten chicken he'd eaten in Spain. He rose and went up to bed, and I cleared the leftovers. I found room enough in the fridge. ∎

Stairway

I'm walking down this street on a Thursday, as I often do, but this was special. The appointment's at four p.m., and this will make all the difference. This was what I hoped for, and I felt the chances were good. More than good: great.

I'd walked this street ever since I'd made it onto my feet with a stumbly toddle, when I still had to go to my hands and knees to get over the curb. Absurd, of course, because then you're not so concerned with where you're going; it's just the going that counts. The point being that I knew this street like the back of my hand.

But today there's something new on the back of my hand. There's a funny jog to the sidewalk. A building juts out and the sidewalk bends around. I never noticed. Some new construction where I'd have to pass through a dark covered walkway and maybe get mugged. Only a jog, but you never know.

And a stairway. An exterior concrete stairway up to another level. Just an option. I could follow the sidewalk under the covered walkway or climb the stairs. There's surely a *Down*. What am I seeing up there? A cluster of lights. It gets dark early now. It must be a new commercial clump, small shops, boutiques, stuff that might add new color to my life. I have plenty of time. I climb the stairs.

I climb the stairs. Steeper than it looks. The shops are aglow but shuttered. Flowers in large terracotta pots, tall white calla lilies with swarms of yellow daisies at their roots. Nice they have flowers whose names I know.

But no way down. Still plenty of time, and this is a special day. A second flight leads me upward from the shuttered boutiques. These are corporate offices—huge lobbies, tile floors, carnivorous vegetation held in check by security guards. Glass elevators run up and down the outside of the skyscraper's skin. We're talking skyscraper now.

Third level, a solitary pigeon waddles thoughtfully, plucking scraps off the bare concrete, muffin crumbs and bits of burrito. I never imagined a pigeon this high. Nor the homeless: I spot a blanketed figure asleep in a doorway, and other clumps in various states of decay—one snoring with his mouth wide open like a birdie wanting a worm.

The appointment's at four p.m. and I'm headed the right direction as long as I find the way down. I could go back, but they always say go forward. I might have stopped back at the cute boutiques, but they never posted their hours. I might have taken the elevator straight up the skyscraper's skin. I might have done the simple jog and ignored the stairs. I might have gone to market to buy a fat pig, come home again jig-a-ti-jig. Hard to think where I was going at the start, what I needed to do, though I still knew it was the big break, the chance of a lifetime, the well-deserved turning point. I only knew that I'd have to make the climb. By the time I got there I'd know.

The stairs keep leading upward. Top of the flight, I see a bunch of hoodlums. They couldn't be hoodlums, this isn't the neighborhood for hoodlums, though at this altitude it's probably not the same hood. But I'm closer now, and they're all wearing angel garb. Men and women, all in business suits with feathers. It's the feathers that say angels.

The concrete is pebbly here, a copper color, golden if the sun slants right, and the landing opens out to a plaza. The hoodlum angels are marble statues, along with famous others: the giant clothespin, the fabric burger, the three plastic hats—a celebration of common things. This might be the topmost level. It might be for this that I climbed the stairs. Or, no, the song—

Stairway to heaven...

I was in high school, with Cynthia in her room, hearing the song and mulling what the lyrics meant. Or in Chicago with Michael at the bar, or Cleveland and someone with me... That whole song of spread-out question marks.

Far distant, I see steps going up. More steps, forever. There might be a clutch of real angels, not these corporate types, gathered to tell me what those lyrics mean. I can only keep climbing the stairs, up and up. But I have to recall that this is only a detour to where I'm really going. ▪

A Visit to Life

You were in the neighborhood, and you just walked into the house of a total stranger. It seemed the thing to do. A woman came out from the kitchen, hugged you as if she expected you and sat you down to supper, nursing from her breast. You weren't sure quite what to say. She seemed to know who you were, or who she wanted you to be, though she didn't have a clue.

You slept in the crib for a while, and they seemed happy to have you as a guest, though sometimes they acted upset when you screamed. Then you got out and learned to balance and talk. After a while they gave you a ride to a place where you had to learn two plus two. You were there a long time, maybe years, but you did learn two plus two and other stuff. Then they gave you a shove out the door and said you should get a job.

You got a job where you put two things with two things but only got three, so you had to do it all over again till it worked. You did it for many years, but whatever you did it was never enough. It always came out the same. Somewhere along that time you were walking up the walkway, and someone was walking beside you. You were walking very close together, almost as if you thought you knew this stranger, or you would.

So you got a new house together and found some nice chairs to sit in. You found a bed to sleep in. After a while, someone showed up at the door, a total stranger, came into the house as if they owned it and screamed, which seemed the thing to do for strangers walking into the house. But soon, much too soon, they went off to learn two plus two.

And then you were old. You could tell just by the mirror, if you put on your glasses first. Or your balance.

You sat in the doctor's office a while, and then the doctor said it's time. You weren't sure if he was talking to you, but he was pointed at you. So it seemed, yes indeed, it was time.

This was an eventful visit to Life. Even though there were all sorts of things you intended to see, like China and the Venice Bienniale. Somewhere you had snapshots that you hoped to sort through, but there comes an end to all things, and it was time to go home. If you remembered the way. ∎

Who Died

Did you see who died?
—Who?

—Carolyn Arliss. She was in some sit-com in the Nineties.

—Well, people do.

—You need to be a franchise to avoid it. Like James Bond.

—Then you're played by different actors.

~

The longer you live, the more people die. It seems that way anyway. Not that we're responsible. They just die.

~

—Marilee Lewis died.

—Jim Turner died.

—Lucia Phelps died.

—Autumn died. Remember Autumn? We met her in Des Moines. Tall redhead, kinda fucked up. She gave you a pair of shoes that didn't fit, but you used them in a show.

—Michael died. Like Steve, I think. Alcohol. So sad.

~

You can't help wondering who's writing your story, lame as it is? Who pops in at the end and squeals, *That's all, folks!*? Could you register a complaint? Make a stink?

~

—George Bartenieff died. He was an actor. I saw him once on stage.

—There's never a shortage of actors.

—But this wasn't some sitcom star from the Nineties. He was a major force in the Off-Off-Broadway scene.

—Which is like a major force in the politics of Luxembourg.

—That whole scene was hugely important.

—Things are important if they're important to someone who's important.

—People dying. It's getting to be like a pile-up on the Santa Monica Freeway.

—Happy trails to us.

~

At a certain point you worry about what kind of mess you'll leave behind, all the loose ends to be tied. All the crap, the knick-knacks, keepsakes, trinkets, flotsam and jetsam, curios, junk. Who even knows how to get a dead friend off Facebook? It keeps showing your birthday when you're dead.

~

—Did you see who died?
—Who?
—Sharon.
—Sharon Spiese?
—Yes.
—Oh.

~

They add up. Cecile, Joan, Leon, Bob, Erika. Not to mention the mothers and fathers, the cousins and aunts, all the ones you might expect to die, which they do, in a hospital bed or getting shot or just sitting there watching the news. They run to escape the swoop of the scythe, and they cover the western sky.

~

—Amazing. Each galaxy the new telescope sees looks like a star, but it's billions of stars.

—Right. I know.

—What somebody said: Life forms persist till their complexities prove fatal.

—Interesting.

—We're fashioned from billions of stars.

—How does that follow?

~

We want to ask, like Emily in the play, to spend just one day more to see the flowers or watch the sun in the trees, before we go back … up the hill … to the grave. I saw that play in high school.

~

—So where are you headed for coffee?

—The usual. ▪

Happy

One morning I woke up happy. Better indeed than waking up as a giant bug or waking up dead, yet I was baffled. I had slept my usual sleep, gyrating like a Roto-rooter, twisting the covers into a tight burrito, I'd dreamt my usual dream, some endless task—sorting bulk mail, peeling garlic, clipping the nails of the cat—and awoken enough to know I wasn't really doing it. No seductive dreams to cling to, no exciting plans for the day, just the same soggy yearning for the day when I might have some exciting plans. And yet I was suffused with happiness.

How to define happy? No trudging for miles with gobs of mud on your feet? No waiting for the Angel of Death to open the seventh seal? No defining the state of your head by what it's not?

But just a kind of chemical contentment. Some sweet diluted honey suffusing my frame the way adrenaline does. Or a liquor that doesn't insist on wobbling the beast too fiercely. Or gentle sunshine.

Like any deep anxiety, of course, I tried to discern its cause. What induced it? How long would it last? Might there be side effects? The cause might be only a blur, but nothing to worry about. I didn't really have to know.

I did my morning things and still felt happy. I started to write a story about my childhood, very sad, but the words fell easily into place—neither too scrawny nor bulgy—and I felt happy. I cleaned the cat pan with a flourish.

Of course I knew that it wouldn't last, that my head wouldn't allow it, that life would come knocking with its cold stone fist. I wasn't a new mother nursing my infant or a kid in the fling of first love or a sky diver gulping free-fall to the very last drop, and yet it was late morning and I still felt happy.

I took a break, logged onto the Web, knowing that would bring me back to normal. News, posts from friends, political diatribes, all the day's atrocities made me recall the song of the platoon marching into the swamp. That was a long time ago, almost yesterday. I saw a post in bold cursive, against an orange backing, directing us to *Eat Shit and Die*, then logged onto a screed saying the same in 5,000 words. But I couldn't break out of my cheer.

I knew that I had no right to be happy. That it was an unfair privilege of my race, my gender, my sexual prefer-ence, my being a citizen of an imperialist power, of being two-legged, both legs working, and other privileges I could not have been aware of since I was irretrievably privileged. I granted that no one should be happy until everyone was, that billions lived in hunger, getting blown apart at random, wondering why they'd ever had kids. I vowed to despair the devastations of climate change. Yet I couldn't manage it.

As the day trickled on, I began to regain normalcy. Af-ter my midday nap I was almost back to my usual funk. Yet again, with my second glass of cheap red wine at wine-time, it returned like the incoming tide. I turned off the news and I danced.

In the coming days, I longed for the expected ending to this tale, where I fell back into the slough of misery. Yet I couldn't break free from my incredulity. I felt happy. ∎

Turnips

Another mass shooting, on the eve of Thanksgiving. We might do better as turnips.

I was rolling my cart through the veggie section of Fircrest Market when another shopper mentioned it to her husband. I always get nervous there, since they separate the organics from the toxics. I fear getting cancer from the cheap stuff, but what if the expensive stuff is just a scam? Can you put full trust in anyone except your mom? You could die from being a dupe. Or from just being shot.

That morning I'd heard other news. A famous actor had died, as they tend to do, or at least somebody who'd been on TV. Some war was dragging on, with another revving up. Homelessness was getting better or worse. Earth was on life support, the Doomsday Clock ticked closer, and a dozen more school kids had died for the right to bear arms. Looking at the bin of Fircrest turnips, I thought about the options.

Turnips gave you comfort. Round simple things, they spurred no ravenous urges, they just lay there. You could let them stay bland or spice them up, but no one was ever moved to exclaim, "Omigod, what exquisite turnips!" No expectations of stardom, and they were pretty cheap.

Someone had posted on Facebook that the electorate had the brains of a turnip. Yet why not? If the human race ever found its true nature, what new age might dawn? No turnip has ever shot children dead or fed them lies. No turnip ever robbed a bank or sped through stoplights. No turnip ever tortured a fellow turnip or posed a threat to life on Earth.

Certainly we'd have less racial strife. Turnips come in different varieties, even colors—tints of red, yellow, and orange—but the common variety, white with a bit of purple, is the most common. If we were all whitish purple, there'd be fewer problems with color, though granted we might have tiffs with the rutabagas.

True that some turnips, or humans posing as turnips, have run for high public office, and some have gotten elected, but most have wound up either roasted or in a boiling pot.

Granted, the technology would be tricky. Yet if we could achieve scientific advances that threaten all life on Earth, we could surely conquer turnips. We might even find a means whereby we could shoot, peel, slice, or boil our fellow veggies, though that might defeat the purpose.

And granted, we'd have to relearn the process of reproduction. It was hard enough in our teens to navigate the channels, but going through all that again—*how does she feel, why doesn't he ask?*—would be hell. Still, how can we say what's hell for a turnip? It might be only when the cook hasn't set the timer.

Most of us feel a sick disgust at being human, the curse of being any race, any gender, an oppressor or a victim, of bearing some culpability in wiping out life on Planet Earth. Yet no one has ever charged a turnip with genocide, much less Original Sin. Turnips get a free pass. Who wouldn't go to extremes to get a free pass?

I remember the old movie *The Thing*. You couldn't kill it because it was James Arness playing an alien carrot. You could only crisp it, so they zapped it with all-electric cookery. And so with the human race. If we all became turnips, there's no guarantee of existence: too many doors for the Angel of Death to pop through. The day would come when a scrawny monk in Tuscany chanced on a Latin recipe for brewing a turnip liqueur.

But just a chance thought as I wheeled past the veggie bins. I picked up a five-pound sack of non-organic potatoes, knowing full well that we're all going to die. The news told me that, if I hadn't already known it. ▪

Near M.I.T.

I live with a man who tries to change Planet Earth. I sleep with him. We have a child. We have money, we have our health, and we've celebrated our twelfth anniversary. I have not the slightest notion what he does.

We met as students. I was psychology, Ed was computers. We mostly talked about our profs' eccentricities. He had a great comic sense, doing these imitations. And we both liked music and skiing. We still ski, or two years ago we skied.

Ed was into cybernetics, robotics, then biochemistry, genetic engineering. I couldn't understand a word, so we both agreed not to talk science. But he'd do imitations of the staff, and I'd laugh. He still had that comic sense.

After college we stayed in Cambridge for his graduate work. We delayed kids, realizing that marriage takes time for the knowing. Cambridge is beautiful, but it's not Omaha, where I grew up. There, they don't change Planet Earth.

And we had a child. Named after his father, but we call him Eddie, of course. Ed's father was Edward, and family traditions are meaningful. My dad's name is Barnett, Barney for short. That's Omaha.

Eddie—our son, I mean—is my center. Not Ed's. His work is his center: changing Planet Earth. I have no notion what he means by that.

The first time, he said it like a joke. He was looking tense, a brick wall between us, and after dinner I asked him, "Hey, could you fill me in? You've been kinda weird."

"We're going to change Planet Earth," he said.

"I'm serious."

"So am I."

That night when he came to bed he was like somebody else. A different rhythm of breathing, a different smell. That morning, after he left for work, Eddie Junior was at camp, so I drifted back to sleep, then I woke stark awake. Sometimes I have terrible dreams.

We've been careful over the years to have time together. His work demands frequent absences, but when we have time I tell him my feelings. It's my role to have the feelings. We never talk about how he feels about what he does.

I'm scared, but it's all a blur. It's the blurry things that scare me. I'm terrified what happens tonight. Ed will be home.

I used to love seeing the papers on his desk when he brought stuff home. Of course the equations and jargon were all Greek to me, but they had an elegance. But now—

"It is forbidden."

"Ed, that sounds totally weird. Do they all talk stilted like that?"

"That's the wording. I'm quoting. It's explicit. It is forbidden."

When Eddie started school I began to work part-time: Good Bodies, a little vitamin boutique. Just to have stuff to say. I'd carry the dinner talk, describe the customers, though I couldn't mimic the way he used to. He works with people who have no eccentricities.

They test you for eccentricities. And the spouse. Very personal questions about my dreams. I soft-pedalled the nightmares. I must have passed. Ed got moved to the next rank inward.

We were having dinner once, Eddie was out at Cub Scouts, we were eating a chocolate mousse, and suddenly

I screamed. I screamed that I did not know him, that we only fuck in the dark. "What's the secret?" I screamed. He ate a spoonful. I knew the answer. They were changing Planet Earth.

One thing about saying we fuck in the dark: I never say *fuck*. But I think the word *fuck* because that helps me fuck. I thought once I should get a tattoo, maybe put me more in the mood. If we ever had some light to see it.

Eddie's sleeping over tonight with Theo, one of his Cub Scout buddies. What might happen tonight? Ed's papers might tell. Once he said, with a dreamy wonder, "Equations tell a story. They're like literature." He's so far out of my league with brains. A mistake for us both.

But I believe him. I believe his job is *Change Planet Earth*. From what to what? It might be something good, like if cars made music instead of the freeway roar, but Ed can't stand music now. How would he know the change is one we want?

I think he would like both me and Eddie dead. I'm startled to think it, but he needs the focus. He'd certainly grieve, but for food he could order carry-out. He had left out a paper on his desk. The secret equations, I knew. I put my finger upon it, and the black squiggles scurried off on a thousand legs. If I had eccentricities, boy, who knows?

I went into Old Times Gone, this antique shop, for an anniversary present. Ed will give me chocolates. He always remembers. He's good that way. I might give him something old and say, "This is the way that it was."

Lots of old knickknacks there, a Coca-Cola sign, a globe where countries had old names like Rhodesia, a sausage grinder… My grandma talked about ice picks. Long spike with a grip. The iceman delivered a block of ice, and you'd chip it to fit. Now you only see them in horror flicks, but they had one at Old Times Gone.

So Ed came home from his trip. Eddie's still at camp, and he'll return to a world that's changed. We'll eat. We'll put on music, then turn it off. We'll go upstairs to fuck.

My dreams always start in the heart or the belly. Two nights ago, I dreamt I was Planet Earth, and when I stood naked I saw it. The faint forms of continents glowed in my skin. I saw it under the blur. Seeing its edges sharp, it held no terror now.

We're in the bedroom. In the light I go naked to Ed. He looks surprised. I brush one hand over my breasts, my stomach, my thighs. In my other hand I hold the Old Times Gone. I am the naked Planet Earth.

I go for the eye. ▪

On TV

I remember when my father first let me watch the war on TV. I was eight, and I'd been asking, but Mom said I was too young. Splatter movies were okay because they were clearly fake. "No, he's old enough," said Dad. Even though I wasn't.

It was Saturday afternoon. Not the usual time that I watched TV, but that's when it got the best ratings. "Want something to nibble on?" Dad said. "No, thanks." Dad got up from his chair and switched the TV to flat. "Why can't we see it in 3-D?" I asked. "Not the first time," he said. I was sitting on the floor leaning against the sofa. Ragsie curled up beside me, and I scratched him on his muzzle.

The field was like a grassy tennis court. People in uniforms were lined up, and there were two flags. The live audience in the stands was quiet, not like a football game, where you cheered for your team, but this was different. There was music playing. The two fighters met in the middle of the field and shook hands.

This one is America, Dad said, but others are worldwide. That's a good thing, he said, it's culturally diverse.

The one fighter wore a bright orange suit. He was huge, big belly and beard and light brownish skin, and his hair was slicked-back greasy. The fat man looked mean. We want to make his country free, the way we are, said Dad.

The other fighter was our President, the ruler of America. He was in an olive-colored uniform like Boy Scouts, but not with the Boy Scout hat. Dad said our President was young and strong and had already won three wars. He looked like a movie star.

They flashed to playpens of little kids at either end of the field, with fences to keep them in. They were all naked, toddling around. Some were little boys and some were little girls. "Thirty pound limit," said Dad.

It started. Each fighter took a little kid out of the separate pens and did like with clubs or baseball bats. They grabbed the ankles and swung and smashed the other guy. Our President won it with only three or four kids.

I got sick. "Maybe your mom was right," Dad said, "you're a little too young for that." "No," I said, "Mom made yams for lunch and they made me sick." "Well, anyway," he said. That night I had a nightmare, but I kept wanting to see the war again. Next day was Sunday, and we watched another, this one from Africa.

In school they'd said in the old days they had spears and swords, and then guns, and then tanks and missiles, and then the nuclear bomb. So why did they use little kids? "It's a long story," Dad said. That meant he wasn't going to tell it. But he told some.

"It takes people a long time before they learn to be … more nice. We had kings for thousands of years before we invented democracy. And fought wars where millions got killed for hardly any reason. People said that the leaders who decide to go to war should be the ones to fight it. Which people thought was silly until they realized it was true. Their own sons and daughters went off to war, got killed, and their countries spent trillions of dollars on weapons while people starved. War was not the answer.

"But you still had to have it if you couldn't agree on stuff. So nations that had the nukes wrote up the rules, then the others had to agree. And even the biggies agreed to follow the rules, though they still kept nukes just in case."

Rules were that the chief executives faced off, and their only weapons were kids under three or less than thirty pounds. I felt sick again. "But why little kids? Why don't they have a fist fight?" It was the toddlers that made it so awful.

"Because war is terrible," Dad said. "War has to be terrible, and you've just seen it. What you see is the true cost of war. Who'd watch it otherwise? We're making it terrible at less cost. What if we did like we used to do, sent off millions of boys and girls, eighteen or twenty or thirty years old, and they've all got people who love them, even babies of their own, and they come back with their faces and arms blown off or in bags. We were doing the same thing as now, only with hundreds of thousands instead of half a dozen. This feels more terrible, sure, but is it?"

I'd dawdled over my cereal and now the flakes were too soggy. "What about the little kids?" I don't know if I was really asking a question.

"They're helping out their families. There's compensation. The cable companies pay it. There's a waiting list."

"Is there one next week?"

"One what?"

"A war."

"We'll check the listings."

It took some getting used to. There's a difference between true horror and entertainment horror, and it's hard to spot the difference. I must have been almost ten before we switched to watching it in 3-D. Only then did Ragsie get up and bark.

For me, it's our duty to watch, like voting for the President who's the best killer. We see the spray of the blood: it's the price that's paid. Like eating yams for lunch, you eat what's in front of you. That's what I tell my kids. ∎

A Hero

Connie Westerly taught fourth grade at James Garfield School in Arlington, Virginia. She was forty-two, divorced, and subject to bouts of depression. As a child she'd dreamed of being Jackie Onassis, but settled for less.

She kept a loaded semi-automatic pistol on her nightstand. She'd had lessons, understood the dangers both accidental and intentional, kept a suicide hotline number in large print beside it, but she couldn't sleep otherwise.

She loved the kids, of course, but kids were kids. They were wild on Monday, bad on Tuesday, though by Thursday and Friday they'd lost all hope of fomenting a jailbreak and resolved to serve out their sentence. But today was Monday again. It seemed to be unavoidable. She fed the cat, made coffee, ate her granola, and finished dressing. Chilly today, so she wore a light jacket with large pockets. She slid the pistol into a pocket, no notion why, except that there'd been three shootings in Tennessee the week before.

Fourth period, David Wertz sat in the front. He had some kind of condition that caused his frequent absence, and she welcomed every minute that he wasn't in the classroom. Connie wasn't religious, no belief in God, but she'd always suspected there was a Satan, and some children, she was convinced, had already signed a pact to bedevil humankind. They made your job unpleasant, pointless, sometimes sheer hell. She saw David Wertz come in, sit at his desk, smile at her, and spit on the floor.

Sharp inhale, and she'd pulled the pistol from her light jacket pocket and fired. It hit the portrait of George Washington at the back of the room. David must have done it. It was just like him. She couldn't wait. She had to protect the class. She held the gun with both hands, aimed, and blew a hole in the child.

Almost before the class began to scream, Connie Westerly was cut down by a hail of bullets from the doorway. Over the clamor came a shout of "Oh shit!" The bled-out teacher slumped on her desk.

Police appeared in a whisk and took eighteen-year-old Gregory Childress into custody. He readily confessed his intent to murder the class and go on to a record-breaking spree, having dreamt of the spree since the age of twelve. Every boy needs a spree. The district attorney weighed possible charges, but declined to call a grand jury. The boy had saved the class from a teacher gone berserk, and you don't prosecute a hero.

Not for another three years did Gregory Childress achieve his long-nourished ambition. ▪

Hell

It was just after five o'clock, and the world was going to hell. I was having my glass of wine before fixing dinner, or something I called dinner since Judith died a year ago. I'd listened to the news at the top of the hour. A chronic mistake, but I felt it was every citizen's duty to suffer the agonies of staying informed.

Last May I retired from the Wisconsin Dept. of Motor Vehicles, doling out licenses to the road-rage multitudes. I could truly claim that for thirty years I had worked to save Planet Earth by encouraging humanity to exterminate itself behind the wheel. For every license I issued, I had saved a redwood, a prairie dog, or a whale.

Retirement brought on loneliness, not to mention ads for burial plots. Since Judith died, I was condemned to suffer my own bland company and cookery. And so I undertook what millions of unfulfilled souls have undertaken: to write a novel. I was trying to craft a thriller, though nothing thrilled me. I was now plodding through the bog of Chapter Two.

I sit at the kitchen table with my laptop. I warm up the leftovers of the leftovers. I try not to think why I'm adding one more story to the multitudes, the way astronomers keep discovering galaxies when they don't know what to do with the ones we've got. I'll juggle my electrons with aplomb and then induce about six friends to claim they'd skim my deathless prose. True, I'd achieve wider readership if I just told it to the feral cats that come begging in the patio. Right now, the world is going to Hell and the brakes won't hold, but I still go tap tap tap.

But I couldn't help thinking, *Hey, a writer's life for me!* Maybe I'd get invited to parties in Manhattan and snarf free food. Or my high school classmates would exclaim, *Omigod, Freddie went to Lincoln High!* Or sexy Cynthia, who stood me up on a date, would give me a call, though by now she's either in her seventies or stone dead. So many astonishing things could happen with this novel, if anyone ever reads it. If I finish it. If I ever get through Chapter Two.

I was on a roll. I had just written *Kilroy whirled around and couldn't believe what he saw.* Then I heard a tortured cry: either a feral cat's howl or a tenor sax solo from the Angel of Death. Then a series of pops like little kids stomping on bubble wrap or the first volleys of the death squads.

My hero Kilroy was staring at the kitchen wall. It had started to burn from inside, just a small brown spot over the photo of Judith, then it grew, and I saw the flames licking the cracks of the wall like the methodical tongue of a feral cat. Kilroy watched to see what it did. Suddenly the wall burst into flame.

It must be what I'm writing. I had flung my vision onto the astral plane, and all Hell broke loose. I never knew the power of my prose. I saw that only I could turn back the fires. I might write something less incendiary, perhaps a children's book, a sequel to *See Spot Run.* Or something hopeful that offered a future without the gnawing of rats. Or stay with my hero Kilroy. In a flash, he splashed his vodka gimlet into the holocaust. Or was vodka flammable?

I stopped typing, fled out the back door, and watched as the outer wall was engulfed in flames. Through the timbers, I caught glimpses of more walls burning. Yet what would hold up the roof? A conundrum: could I safely ignore the flames? Would they go dormant, as Judith did as she sat there after lunch? And where were the feral cats? Afire?

I must have set this raging blaze. But how? I didn't smoke. I'd once left the burner on when I was frying eggs, but that only made a stink, not the flames of Hell that were burning the attic where mementoes of Judith—journals and photos and tax reports—were stored. Perhaps merely writing *the flames of Hell* was sufficient to evoke an inferno. Could I write *the soothing rain* and all would again be well?

The house collapsed before me, but I was untouched for now. Not unlike the houses I'd lived in over the course of time that no longer stood. And most of the past was gone: Judith, the job, all the books, a little sparkly crystal I'd bought in Camden—long story. Odd that I'd felt no heat, but perhaps that was an advantage of age: you go numb.

Fire insurance might pay, if insurance still existed, given the massive collapse of life as I'd known it. I might look out the window, if I could find any windows that weathered the fall, and see nothing for miles except rubble and smoke. It might be that Kilroy was lost amid the swirling miasma, signaling through the flames.

Maybe Hell wasn't a place you go to: maybe it comes to you. ▪

Night

Breathe in, breathe out.
Breathe in, breathe out.
Good, simple. Just do that a while.
It's three a.m. or something and my mind is running on
politics or how I deal with the crap I'll leave when I'm
dead or what's the meaning of life unless I get a good
night's sleep—
Breathe in, breathe out.
Breathe in, breathe out.
Think of my breath, what they say, just let it all go, or turn
on the light to see if it's three a.m. but I'll scream if it's
three a.m. so just breathe.
Breathe in, breathe out.
Breathe in, breathe out.
How long?
Breathe like a horse, big horse that breathes in, breathes
out, and you curry the horse, wash its dick, what a horse-
lover learns they have to do, but saddle it, put it in gear,
step on the gas and ride it to town— But stop with the
fucking horse and the monkey mind!
Breathe in, breathe out.
Breathe in, breathe out.
And they're training the goon squads, guys on the corners
with guns that call you a candy-ass—
Breathe in, breathe out.
Till we have to start packing the van and move to Chicago, Philly, Baltimore, even at three a.m.

Breathe in, breathe out.
Breathe in, breathe out.
The birds…
If they pick up the trash on the Fourth…
The swan…
Is there even a point where you pack the van and the van
is full but there's still the futon, the boxes of books, all the
files and the photo albums, all the shit you accumulate,
the bins of puppets, the kitchen utensils, the tools, the
spices, the two-by-fours, the ceremonial robes, the bells—
Forgot to breathe but is there even a point…
Breathe in, for chrissake, breathe out.
And you die, you'll be dead, you'll lie there and stink and
your kids have to deal with this crap, this double lifetime
of crap, and hire help to haul it away to the city dump and
how will they feel, how will they ever know…
The little glass swan we got in Venice, amazing how…
Breathe in, breathe out.
We need coffee beans, wine, vodka. But the van starts up,
it's driving backwards, you watch in the rearview mirror
what's coming, what your back is crashing into—
Breathe in, breathe out.
Breathe in, breathe out.
Am I drifting off?
Breathe in, breathe out.
Call it the monkey mind. but monkeys don't ride horses
or vans. Monkeys don't care about politics, they don't care
about dying or all the banana peels they accumulate over
a lifetime, or think about not being here…
Breathe in, breathe out. Am I asleep?
Maybe some music would help. ■

The Death of Howdy Doody

I was the puppet that brought TV into the capitalist era. *Howdy Doody Time!* That name would leap into the hearts of a million geezers and sink in its claws. The Peanut Gallery, Buffalo Bob, Mr. Bluster, Dilly Dally, the Flub-a-Dub, and Clarabell! Clarabell with his honker blatting and seltzer squirter, pandemonium, the kids all screeching like weeny berserkers. Then, center stage, Howdy Doody, jiggling his little tuchus: good versus evil, calm amid chaos, a wooden smile and non-stop words from our sponsor.

Oh how they loved Howdy Doody, watched him every day, 3:30 Eastern, 4:30 Central. They bought Howdy Doody wristwatches, Howdy Doody cowboy suits. They prayed for Howdy Doody. His calcified rictus reigned until 1960, when America began its disintegration.

But what a fake! I was more real, more comic, more like real people, and the world might have been better off. But they murdered me.

No question but they loved that pimply red-headed all-American twerp. They thought that was Howdy Doody, but I knew the truth. They kept nothing more of me than the way I tilted my head when I was trying to think, and the name.

It was all a question of copyright. Howdy was an American icon, and American icons are owned. Mickey Mouse is owned, Michael Jackson is owned, the U.S. Senate is owned— No politics though. I'm past all that. Unstrung, drawn and quartered, charred and forgotten.

In 1949, a puppeteer brought a case against the Howdy Doody Show. It had started on the radio in Buffalo—hence "Buffalo" Bob Smith, who did all the voices. When TV came in, the producers found a puppeteer with lots of circus puppets, including me. When the show became a hit, he wanted a cut of the royalties from cereal boxes, candy bars, doodads and gizmos. But they said no, so he picked up his puppets and walked, including the star, myself, whose original name was Elmer.

This bears explanation. I began as Elmer, but Bob always started the show with me hooting, "Howdy Doody, boys and girls!" So they started calling me Howdy. I liked Elmer better. Of course that was a name reserved for goofy guys, but I was a goofy guy, sporting a big toothy smile, ears sticking out like rear-view mirrors, exuding a low-class scrounginess. My jaw was too long, my forehead squarish, with reddish scrub-brush hair, daubed-on eyebrows and crossed eyes. My vest shrank my chest and my cowboy chaps blossomed out like bloomers. But still I didn't mind Howdy. It sounded friendly.

Success requires redesign, I guess. So they bandaged my head and told the kids that Howdy was having a face-lift. The storyline was that Howdy was running for President of the Kids of America, and kids wanted a handsome guy, not a goofy guy. So the producers commissioned a new design, and with a big fanfare they stripped off the bandages, and there he was: freckles, red hair, cowboy suit, big watermelon smile. Sunrise in America.

The lawsuit dragged on and was settled out of court for a substantial sum, peanuts compared to the millions raked in throughout Doodyville and its subsidiaries. But a condition of the settlement was this: *Our clients require that the original so-called Howdy Doody does not reappear and assert claims to be the original Howdy Doody, which would compromise the integrity of the iconic Howdy Doody and the associated licensing rights.*

It specified dismemberment and incineration of the original marionette, which might create an identity crisis for the franchised entity. The auto-da-fe was to be witnessed by both lawyer teams. A custodian had placed a heavy towel on the oval walnut conference table, then a flat bed of bricks supporting a barbecue grill, with a portable fan for ventilation. Dead men would tell no tales.

It was the hour of the burning. The box was opened, the strings drawing me forth. I was five minutes from being erased, condemned by consent decree. Above me, a flickering fluorescent, which I saw as my soul blinking on and off. The lawyers were standing around, some giggling at the absurdity, or maybe at the butt-ugly elf who was me. I tried to do a little dance, but they'd scissored my strings. I closed my eyes so no one would see my nakedness. I was clipped apart at the joints and stacked on the grill. I smelled the tang of charcoal starter, and my fingers twitched. At last my eye paint curled in the flame and my teeth were afire. My smile persisted. Nothing could mar the joy of Elmer "Howdy" Doody.

If I'd stayed with the show, who knows? Maybe there wouldn't have been the assassinations, the civil rights killings, Vietnam—maybe kids would have grown up goofier. Or maybe I was just entertainment, something to sell merchandise, nothing more.

All the millions of kids, they got what was left. Howdy Doody lunch box, cookie jar, squeeze toy, galoshes, ear muffs, piggy bank, official Howdy Doody Junior Firefighter's Badge...

This was actual fact. It's in a book. ∎

The Muffin Man

Usually, when I go to the gym, I take my iPhone along to blow music into my head or hear an edifying podcast. But sometimes I forget to charge it, and it plays two measures of Beethoven and gives up the ghost. Then I have to torture my abs or my glutes and listen to the crap they play over the speaker system. If all else fails to get you through the three rounds of twelve heaves each, you have to start to think.

Normally, I can avoid thinking at least till noon, when I can put it off during lunch and a nap after lunch. If I were in a high-paying executive job, I could avoid it altogether. But today at the gym, I was forced into it. My mind fumbled around in those dear dead days beyond recall, and came up with the muffin man.

> *Oh do you know the muffin man*
> *The muffin man, the muffin man*
> *Do you know the muffin man*
> *Who lives in Drury Lane?*

Why did this manifest in my consciousness? If the levels of quantum reality opened to let slip the silliest songs through the door like frantic cats, why could I not come up with *How Much Is That Doggie in the Window* or *Purple People Eater* or *Alvin and the Chipmunks* and countless other manifestations of Western Civilization?

Once again I tried my iPhone before I launched into the Upper Thoracic Spreader, but the battery was down to zilch. I was stuck with the muffin man.

It had become an earworm almost instantly, and its only qualification was that it was surely the dumbest song we'd ever sung in grade school. It may have had a hidden meaning, like other nursery rhymes. The muffin man may have been the Prime Minister, a murderer who poisoned his wife with doctored English muffins, or a famous male prostitute in Soho, but we sang it as if we knew.

I shifted to a machine that would strengthen my calves. I rather liked torturing my calves. They were farther from me than my arms, or they were felt to be. But now it started to become clear. I recalled the second verse:

> *Oh yes I know the muffin man*
> *The muffin man, the muffin man*
> *I do know the muffin man*
> *Who lives in Drury Lane.*

That was an absolute lie. None of us knew the muffin man, yet we sang it out as if he was our brother and hogged the toilet in the morning when we were needing to pee. We were learning not only to ask something stupid, but to sing out a lie. It was surely indoctrination in the rituals of patriarchy, rampant capitalism, white supremacy, neo-colonialism, all the traditional values.

I think I saw through this scam at an early age, but that didn't exempt me from Cub Scouts, Boy Scouts, or earning my God & Country Award just before I left the church. I didn't believe a bit of the stuff, but I'd worked for the award. But that was all before voting age, so I didn't do any serious harm. I only worry that it's affected me on a very deep level. I'm not much in touch with my very deep level. I always preferred to skim the top. I remember helping my grandma milk the cows, and the cream would rise to the top, where you skimmed it off.

But then I googled *muffin man*, and I learned a lot more. I could never remember where he lived, and I saw it was Drury Lane. There was a famous theatre in Drury Lane, the Drury Lane Theatre, which I knew from my Ph.D. studies. But I never knew the muffin man lived near there. They had never told us that at Stanford.

And I learned that it was a children's game. You stood in a circle. You sang the first verse to the kid on the right, and they sang the *Oh yes* verse. And then you both sang—

> *The two of us know the muffin man*
> *The muffin man, the muffin man*
> *Two of us know the muffin man*
> *Who lives in Drury Lane.*

Then the second little kid—it might have been Kathy Bogardus, who would die before second grade—sang to the third, and then it was *Three of us.* It went on like that, implacably, until we went round the circle, and then we all sang in blessed relief—

> *We all know the muffin man*
> *The muffin man, the muffin man*
> *We all know the muffin man*
> *Who lives in Drury Lane.*

Except we didn't. Not one of us did. We were only folloing orders, singing the goddamned song, preparing the way for the Fascists.

I finished my exercise agenda, twenty minutes or so, and looked forward to my coffee. In the car I turned on the morning news. ▪

Holocaust

She'd gone into a two-week spate of writing haikus. She'd learned that the five-seven-five syllable-count wasn't rigidly adhered to in English, though she couldn't help counting the syllables—always feeling otherwise that she'd peeked at the answers or cheated somehow. There wasn't much money in haikus—you didn't expect one to make the best-seller list—but somehow she found them compelling. Having written a couple of novels, no takers, it was such great relief to write three lines, proclaim "It is finished," and give up the ghost.

This one came out of a Friday morning at Friendly Joe's Espresso, an outdoor coffee stand on the square. She'd written something about sparrows pecking the muffin crumbs on the asphalt, something about the stout barista, confronting the moral judgment inherent in *stout*. Then she saw two old men at a patio table drinking coffee together, and she wrote it.

> *Holocaust*
> *and morning coffee bind*
> *two old friends*

Perhaps it was the oddity of old men together. In most coffee shops, old men clustered in groups, or else they cringed in dismal isolation. It was women like her who sat chatting in intimate duos, though she had little talent for chat. Perhaps that's why she wrote it. She had no interest in *The Holocaust* except as a scar on the face of humanity. Humanity already had plenty of scars.

She'd learned that haikus had spawned journals, mostly online, so she submitted it for publication. All writers want to be heard, so she sent it off, with two other haikus tagging along.

From the editors of *Modern Haiku* or something like that, the two old friends were accepted. The one proviso they added was, "Could you add a *the* to holocaust?"

Holocaust for her meant anything that was horrific in life. Holocaust meant the end of meaning, the end of hope. She had read that *holocaust* referred originally to the ritual sacrifice, burning the whole beast, leaving nothing to the priests or for sale of the meat to the market next day. Holocaust, for her, meant not Hitler's final solution, it meant the lives that splayed out year by year behind the two old men who talked over coffee.

In a sense, the editors' suggestion—*the Holocaust*—made sense. It gave a powerful context to the friendship of the men. Even if they weren't victims, it was a heavy part of their lives. She hadn't intended that, but it was real.

On the other hand, she hadn't intended that. Somehow for her it cheapened the image. It was an easy reference, almost a cliche, something that writers reached for, having no right to claim it but needing to evoke a cheap tear. She mulled it for a day.

On the one hand, it would be a publication credit. On the other, what was the value of a publication credit for a haiku? On the one hand, it was probably a stronger poem if people understood it. On the other, that's not what she'd intended.

Was it just evoking a cliche? She mulled it over, she talked to her boyfriend, she composed a soul-searching letter to the editor which she didn't send. At last she wrote *Sure*. It got printed, or at least posted, with the change. She listed the publication on her credits, for what it was worth.

She never saw the old men again. She had no notion
what they were talking about. It may have been the novels
of Anthony Trollope. It may have been motorcycles, their
wives, their troubles with drain spouts or kidneys. Friendly Joe's Espresso got sold and was now a stand for tacos.
She knew it was bound to happen. ▪

Conundrum

He faced a conundrum. "Why is Shadow so totally fixated on the faucet? Soon as I start to put my lenses in, he jumps up on the sink to stare at the dribble."

"Cat brains are like that," said Lily.

"Then I pull the plug, whoosh down the drain, and he's like *Where'd it go?*"

"Contemplating his own mortality, you think?"

"Or mine."

The issues adumbrated by the cat named Shadow—a recent household addition—perplexed the young professor. Neither his dissertation nor a Stanford seminar in Hegelian tenets nor his years of application to his specialty had prepared him for the riddles posed by a bouncy sphinx. The mystery overcast his morning.

At such times, he wondered why he had ever stepped out of his physics groove to take a philosophy seminar. To broaden his horizons? He didn't want broad horizons— it suggested *fat-assed*. He had joked with Lily, who'd seen him through grad school, about Sartre's scoliosis, Kant's hemorrhoids, Schopenhauer's giggle fits, Karl Marx's obsession with flying kites. Now he couldn't help picturing Kierkegard hopping up to the sink to stare at the dribble in deep Danish funk.

He'd loathed that seminar and only pulled a B. Trying to sleep at night, he had felt a yearning to be a clown and thought of hilarious clown routines. He forgot them by morning.

Now his Intro class: MWF at 10, intro to something, he couldn't say what. "Dr. B, question on Chapter Four?" Marcella again. Would she never stop with the questions?

"We will never fully comprehend."

He got a laugh. The truest words ever spoken, he thought, but her eyes turned to steel, her lips to blades, and her face to stone—the laugh was at her expense. His laugh line was telling her *Your question does not rise past the level of nonsense.* He didn't mean to do that. But how did we truly know the answer to any question? The best minds of millennia had flung themselves against their own ignorance and flopped on the concrete with bruises. Or fatuous flippant word-play.

Still, he had dodged the question, an essential skill for anyone in the teaching profession or presently living on Planet Earth. He would listen to the question, nod his head thoughtfully, and reply that it was an excellent question to consider. He would launch into a shaggy-dog anecdote about Shadow their frizzy cat. He would say, "I'll give that some thought," and forget it instantly. He would say that we'd get to that in coming days. Or he would dismiss it with a joke. Not that he felt embarrassment at his ignorance nor hostility to his students: just that questions became more unanswerable day by day. Why indeed did Shadow stare at the dribble?

At the end of the year he resigned his tenure-track appointment and took a job in the private sector. ∎

Fame

It was Sunday, so they were driving to the ocean, as they did every week. Often, it was warm enough to take their beach chairs and sit outdoors as they picnicked. At times it was chilly or too breezy, so they sat in the car. They could deal with most anything. They'd been through a lot together.

"It's anybody's guess," said Liz as they began the twenty-minute drive.

"But I'm not sure anybody cares." said Theo. "We're not famous." Liz laughed.

But when they pulled into the parking lot at Arched Rock, there was tumult. The lot was full: jeeps, minivans, even a couple of camera trucks from TV news, and a gaggle of reporters—or at least they looked like the reporters in movies.

"Is it a holiday?" asked Theo.

"In June?" replied Liz.

Their car was quickly surrounded. "

Theo rolled down his window. "What's up?"

A dozen voices, all asking questions.

"You're famous!" cried a female voice in a degenerate chirp.

Liz leaned across. "No, you're mistaken, we're not famous, we're just here for a picnic." But she couldn't be heard for the stir.

"We'd better go," Theo murmured to Liz. "They think we're somebody else." He backed and filled to escape. "I'll try Vista Point." Same story, plus a helicopter. Someone was trying to rip off their fender. They decided to go home. It wasn't worth the ruckus.

They pulled into their driveway: a swarm of paparazzi and a line of tourist buses. They abandoned the car and made for the door, with Theo swinging the picnic basket to clear the way. At last they were safe inside. They drew the curtains to shield themselves. The phone was ringing.

After catching her breath, Liz spoke. "Is this like somebody said, we've all got fifteen minutes of fame?"

"I'd prefer cancer," said Theo.

"But what did we do?"

For a while it puzzled them that they had done nothing to warrant this: no best-sellers or gold records, no Olympic medals, no major crimes, no winning the Lottery since they never played it. But they soon realized that you didn't need to do anything. A rat doesn't need to sing *Dixie* to attract the cat. The pigeon flies over, drops his load, and whomever it hits is famous.

They also discovered that "the public's right" was supreme. Third day, someone grabbed their cats for souvenirs.

It wasn't all bad. There was money to be made. Offers came in for endorsements: a lipstick for men, a female jock strap, a bitcoin investment scheme promising instant wealth at no risk, reusable toilet paper. There were lucrative movie offers for their story.

"We don't have any story."

"We'll give you one."

But in two weeks, their problems were solved. The driveway cleared. The phone went dead. Their cats were delivered back and scratched on the door, though the tails were slightly shorter.

"Fame has a short shelf life," said Theo. "Who remembers James Wilson, a prominent figure in writing the

Constitution? He could be a substitute teacher, sixth grade, who eats yogurt for breakfast." Liz laughed.

Next Sunday they went to the ocean. The horizon had dissolved in mist, and the parking lot was bare. They set out their chairs on the cliff above the beach, sipped their sherry, and watched a flight of pelicans through the clouds. Life was back to normal. ▪

Toy Trains

I was six. "You're six!" they'd exclaim, as if I'd done something big, but my half-brother was eighteen and already in the Army. Being big now, I tried to help my mom with the dishes, but I broke a cup. "It had memories," she said. I didn't know what she meant. She tried to glue it together, I guess so the memories would come back.

Saturday, Mom took me shopping for Christmas presents for my sister and my step-dad. My brother wouldn't be home. He was overseas protecting our way of life and never paid much attention to me, except to rumple my hair. Mom always sent him socks.

We went to a big department store. Counters with dresses and make-up and neckties and things I couldn't tell what they were. I could only see the front of the counters, but next year I'd be taller, Mom said. Across the store I saw the counters of toys, but we weren't going there today. My sister wanted a new dress for her Barbie, but Mom said Barbies were a rlpoff. And we'd get a book for my stepdad. "We'll say it's from you," Mom said, even though I couldn't read. "He likes murder stuff," Mom said. "Creepy, but they always solve the case, so I guess it's okay."

The store was crowded with shoppers. She made me hold her hand tight, but suddenly I broke away. In the middle of the store, not in any department but right in the center, I saw a world. I wormed my way up to the edge.

Toy trains. The layout was two or three times the size of Mom's and my stepdad's bed. Not the clunky old Lionel train that Jeremy had in his basement, where you'd watch it go round and round and round like an old dog chasing his tail. That was no fun. But this…

Sleek little trains, two or three running at once on different tracks. A place where cattle got loaded into cattle cars, tiny toy cattle with real plastic hair, and a passenger station with little passengers standing around. Hills with trees descending into valleys, and tunnels through hills where you'd see it go in and never know if it'd come out again and then it did. A town with a block-long Main Street, an old bum on a park bench, a hot dog stand that even had little hot dogs on it, a crossing gate that came down when the train was coming and a garbage truck waiting to cross—you could almost smell the garbage. There was a world up there, so rich, so green. It was all so real you couldn't tell it from real. It was a world so full I could almost get on the train.

I got on the train. The one going east. I was six, but I got on the train and then I was seventeen.

September, 1960. It took me to Chicago. College in Chicago, then I graduated, got married, we moved around—Palo Alto, Atlanta, Milwaukee, Philadelphia—we had an amazing life, plus two kids. Not always an easy ride but more fulfilling than watching Jeremy's clunky old Lionel go around and around the track, and hear him boast that he'd saved up four bucks from his paper route and could buy more track.

We traveled into old age. But then before New Year's I had to go home. I got off at the station where the tiny people waited to catch their trains, and we finished our Christmas shopping. I helped choose a necklace for Sis, and Mom bought a book.

That night at home, Mom told my stepdad about the trains. He shook his head, huffed out a thoughtful huff, and spoke more words than I'd ever heard him speak. "They're phasing it out, the railroads, everything," he said. "It's all trucks now for freight and airplanes to get where you're going. They kill the Indians, so they name a football team for the Indians. They pave over the forests, so they paint pictures of trees." He turned to reading the paper. "Same goes for raiilroads. Toy trains, yep." I wasn't sure what he meant. ∎

What's Hidden

He sits at the bus stop, corner of McKinley and 5th. Earflap cap, wool jacket of no color, big nose, looks to be middle-aged, forty or so. Beside him sits an object the size of square buttocks, covered with a red striped towel.

An old woman appears. Curly red hair, cloth coat of no color, pert nose, looks to be seventy or so. She stands for a time, then impatiently, "You mind? There's no place to sit."

"Oh. Sorry." He stands, offering his seat.

"Well, I— Just move your stuff!" He makes a helpless shrug. "No, is this the old thing of the gentleman offering the lady his seat? I've been through that enough. Grow up!" She turns and hurries on to the next stop.

People don't understand. The man sits and peeks under the towel.

A policeman appears from nowhere, as policemen do. Cop hat, pug nose, uniform a colorless blue—life was colorless today. Hand is on his holster. He speaks with lethal politeness, "Sir, we've had a complaint. Lady said you were sitting here in a suspicious manner. Could I see some ID?"

"Why sure." The man rises, starts to reach for his wallet.

"Hold it right there. Keep your hands where I see 'em. What are you hiding? Uncover that object, sir."

"You want me to take off the cover?"

"Right quick, buddy. Do it!" The man starts to lift the towel. "Freeze!" The policeman draws his service pistol, waves it as if swatting flies.

The man wavers. "Officer—"

"Shut up! Talk! Do it! Freeze!"

"Well I mean it's not like a bomb."

"Bomb! He said bomb! He's got a bomb! Backup! Ten-four! May-day! Farewell my wife and children!"

The cop fires three rounds into the air, backs up, trips over a dachshund, shoots at it, misses, runs out into traffic, is hit by a truck, flies into a taco stand, and lies in a heap, crying for his childhood.

The man sits. He takes a breath to pull himself together, then peeks under the towel. He gropes for words, which never come readily.

A derelict stands six feet away. Scraggly beard, stocking cap, wall eye, a pit in the bridge of his nose. Long coat over baggy trousers and a sweater over a plaid shirt over long johns, colorless all.

"Spare change, buddy?"

"Sure. Let me check." He digs in his pocket, takes out a five and some coins, reaches it out to the man.

The derelict backs away. "Whatta you hidin? Don't tell me. Big stuff. Shoppin spree. Presents for the kiddies, goodies for the missus, sexy nightie for your sweetie, gold-plated squeaky toy for your fuckin poodle, and you dig in your pocket for a hand-out, what the fuck I do with a hand-out? I need a decent job! I need a place to live! I need one fuckin reason to stay alive! Time's comin, up against the wall, fuckhead! Fuck you!" He storms off, dragging his life, screaming and kicking, behind him.

A young woman appears. She wears a stylish gray running suit, two cameras dangling on straps down her front. "I saw how you treated that man."

"I was only—"

"Sure, you were trying to be nice. Kind. Fatherly. Right: demonstrate your privilege. Disempower him. Cut off his balls. You are so typical. You are classic. Could I take your picture? What's that?"

"This?" He touches the object beside him.

"Don't tell me. It's your heart. You've commodified your heart. Monetize the teddy-bear, baby-blue with a bright red nose and silver tinsel. It begins to dance in the air and squeak *Hallelujah*. You make me puke." She rushes off to puke. The man puts his hand on the striped towel on the object on the bench.

A bus comes huffing to a stop and the door folds open. A small boy gets off. Red t-shirt, bluejeans, green eyes, the start of a nose, looks to be about six or so. Some color.

"I know what you're hiding," says the boy.

"Do you?"

"Uh-huh."

"How do you know?"

"I'm you."

"Well I'm not hiding it, it's just got a towel over it." The man has had no idea what was hidden under the towel, but he's cared for it thoughtfully. He rises and gets on the bus. The bus heaves away. The towel has red stripes.

The small boy sits on the bench and awaits the next bus. ∎

Pancreas

The endocrine system is like comedy: it's all in the tim-ing. The juice squirts out from the adrenals, pituitary, pancreas, thyroid, to form this exquisite chemical cocktail. Each department sends federal regulators to balance the cells or else the Dow Jones deflates and there's no recovery from recession. It's like juggling balls that change shape as you juggle.

I was directing a show for our theatre in Milwaukee. Two weeks to opening and a scene needed more work—the witches in the laundromat—too slow, more urgent, it's farcical life or death. But something was going askew. Why were the colors changing? Why were the actors blending into the backdrop, Arleen and Flora dissolving into pink and blue?

I saw my actors diffuse like watercolors into the mot-tled curtain. That wouldn't work: we needed to see them clearly. I made a note—*sharper!*—but the pen did a silly scribble, and suddenly I'm up on my feet, knock over my chair, run into the lobby—*But we're in rehearsal!*—slap into a wall, bound up the stairs, through the office, down the stairs four at a time, and actors are yelling, "Ken? What's going on?" Who's Ken? I'm Ken and they're calling my name, but I knock over a bookshelf and run out the front door of the theatre, into the street—*Why am I doing this?*—and fall face flat in the mud.

I'm locked out. They yell my name, but someone's in-side my name, and I'm locked out. My friends come and put me into a car. They think it's me, but I'm locked out and can't find the keys. My wife is holding me close. I have a wife, she plays one of the witches, we've been together twelve years, but I can't remember her name.

I'm in a car, they're taking me for help, but I'm the director. At the ER I see myself jumping up on the gurney, yelling something I can't hear, maybe *Where's my keys?* And they give me a shot that puts me into instant hibernation.

Then the doctor does his doctor things and suggests what's wrong is that I'm an actor so I'm acting out. He clearly thinks it's drugs. My wife takes us to a friend's house to keep us all safe. We sleep on a waterbed.

Three months later, it happens again. Not frantic this time, but one morning I don't wake up. She pries open my mouth and pours honey down my throat to bring my blood sugar up to snuff.

I go to another doctor, who orders a glucose tolerance test. Can I get to the lab early morning, swig this huge glass of green sweet oily phlegm without throwing up? Somehow I manage, and the doctor orders more tests.

We've left our Milwaukee theatre and moved to Chicago. No money, a basement apartment, car exhaust coming in the windows. A two-year-old son, a daughter on the way by C-section, so my wife doesn't get off easy. We're scheduled to produce three new shows, plus a five-week residency in Delaware.

On an afternoon walk, I see her face break out in feathers. Another time it's leather patches in many shades, stitched together by yarn, quite beautiful in fact, but not what I need to see. I want to break open my head. There's somebody in there: not me.

Turns out to be a very rare condition, which the hospital finds intriguing enough to admit me as a research patient room, nurses, doctors, tests, all free. Fortunate, as we have no money. It does involve being given a general physical by every intern and resident on the staff—all races, creeds, and national origins poking fingers up my ass. But for free.

I'm reading in bed late at night, and the TV is on. I look up at these strange cartoons, large mouths chomping, Queen Victoria's head hinged open with a plant sprouting out. I'm hallucinating: should I call the nurse? But at last, no, I'm watching public TV, the first American broadcast of *Monty Python*. It's not me flipping out. It's the world.

But they can't make a definitive diagnosis unless they catch me going bonkers, and then they can take a tell-tale blood sample. So they put me on a fast, and one night, as I'm reading, the words begin to scurry like tap-dancing ants, and then I'm flailing about the bed, and four male nurses are holding me down— *I'm outside with the door locked, I can't find the keys—*

And one nurse comes close to my ear. She whispers low. She knows I'm terrified, she says, but it's okay. She speaks to the me inside me. Then the other nurses do their thing, they suck out my blood, and I sleep.

Next day, the whispering nurse comes in. *How did you know to talk to me?* She tells me of her epilepsy, its control by medication, but her difficulty in getting her nursing license. She knew that within this crazy man there was a me, someone to speak to, someone terrified, someone who needed a friend. She was the friend.

And they discover it's an insulinoma, aha, a tiny growth in the pancreas, very rare, which incites floods of insulin, so my blood sugar falls to zilch and my brain runs off like a waiter pursuing big tips. So what do I do? Just die? The doctor says, no, it's likely benign, so they schedule surgery, but four months from now. With another show to do, I carry a stash of jelly beans to rehearsal, but a few bad times when I forget to munch—terrorists under the bed.

I have the surgery: a huge incision to flop the stomach out of the way and root around for the pancreas, an organ the texture of oatmeal, to find the weensie tumor the size of a pea. Blip, it's out, the blood sugar's up, and my brain works again. The show opens the day before my surgery opens me. The show gets a bad review.

But I'm home. I feel the keys in my pocket. On with the rest of life. ▪

A Blessing

I recall reading some lines of a poem by W.B. Yeats that was new to me. I was lounging in my reading chair, not really wanting to do much, so I poked my laptop onto a poetry blog. They were quoting Yeats, and for some reason I could see him sitting in a Dublin pub, fifty-odd years old, sipping a Guinness, and hearing a jingle of verse in his head. Suddenly he felt the urge to bless the whole world.

It was a poem of blessing. So he wrote the poem, not one of his keepers but the best he could do right then. Decades later, most of a century in fact, I read it. I too had been juggling words, the best I could do right then. But could I feel I was blest or could bless? With news of eighty-five thousand kids starved in Yemen, millions more enrolled for their basic training in death? With refugees facing razor wire? With the oceans dying amid climatic climacteric? In a haystack full of needles, where was the single blessing?

This floated to mind next morning as I drank my coffee. Yeats had written many great poems between the world wars. He died just before second had its premiere, but it was in rehearsal and would go on to rave reviews and winning a dozen Oscars. The headlines scurried like roaches over the face of the Holy Mother. He had surely seen the rough beast slouching, so it must have been a painful stretch for the poet to feel blest or to bless.

Still, things have changed since Yeats. More coffee drinkers in Dublin now, and I can attest that the Arabian blend I drink is better than anything then, as Yeats himself was superior to Kipling or Lanier. Blessings can as soon come as surely as with St. Paul, a lightning bolt knocking him off his horse.

Indeed, humanity might profit by being knocked off our horse, but we're still not quite ready for a tsunami of epiphanies. Best perhaps to take our tiny ecstasies as they come. My wife conjures salads out of fresh earth, and we made children together.

~

Bare hospital room, Denver, October, some unrecorded year. The full-term unborn babe feels the waves of grunts and cries, endures thirty-two hours of a ride of earth tremor and squeeze. Dark tunnel, sudden blast of light, and a fall into frigid hands. The mother's heartbeat now is drowned in the wheeze of machines. The babe knows only that it's born into Hell.

Then it's placed in a strangely familiar embrace of living flesh. It feels the surge of its musculature, then an instinctive urge to nuzzle. It finds the nipple—mindless of demons lurking in October—and sucks.

So you feel the shock of the light, and work your way to the nipple. ∎

The Dance

I was trying not to die. I knew I would, probably soon, but so much depended on my holding out. My children, of course, even though they're both grown, and my husband Gerald, who's also mostly past childhood. And the cats. And my neighbor Nancy, whose life is a total trainwreck but she often calls, and I make grunting sounds that seem to help. They'd likely get on without me okay, but I never shake the need to be needed.

The Devil stood at the foot of the couch I was lying on. I chose to lie on the couch, not back in the bedroom. They talked about *deathbed*, never death couch. A bed called forth images of dying in bed, treatments in bed, waking up in a stranger's bed. Of course I had the same IV rack dripping poisons into my arm—God's punishment for all the *Eat your broccoli* orders to the kids at the table. And I felt more comfortable on the couch until I glanced up and the Devil was standing there with his dull dead eyes.

Of course it may have been the doctor—the eyes were the same—but no sign of a stethoscope and he didn't ask me how did I feel. And no doctor made house calls now. He looked bored, so I pointed to a stack of *New Yorkers*. I hadn't read them for weeks but they just kept coming. He must have already known what was what.

I fumbled for my pen and daybook, thinking to make a list. If I had a list of intentions, obligations, daily tasks, I couldn't die till I'd done it. And directives for the funeral—there couldn't be a funeral without directives. And an outline of the term paper I had to write for history class, the last term paper I'd ever have to write. This was forty years ago. I tried to recall the subject. How could I write it if I didn't know the subject? If I failed, I'd die, I knew it. That's what happened to people who failed.

The Devil stood there staring at something over my shoulder, so yes, this might really be the doctor. But he was wearing a white Sam Browne belt, like we did on the school safety patrol. My first year in junior high was the first they'd let girls on the safety patrol. We helped the little kids across the street, and if I died they might get hit by a thundering bus. But how did the Devil get on the safety patrol? Was he only in seventh grade?

They never tell you that dying, just getting dead, takes such a long time. For some it's painful, hopefully not. Always, I guess, the Devil is standing there, in his white Sam Browne belt, waiting for the traffic to clear and let you across. He's not really hungering for your soul, that's too much paper work, but he thinks that you might be lonely.

That was the last I knew I was me. Time slowed to a stop, and I stopped. The Devil was just my husband Gerald, I recognized now, a frail crinkly figure who fell apart when I coughed. My worklist had only one item: just die. So I did. It might have been the cats who missed me the most: they thought I was their mama because I fed them and hugged them tight.

But I had my dance with the Devil. I'd always held the image of having a final dance. It could as readily be with God, but his beard might get in the way. But the Devil could be my husband Gerald or the doctor or almost anyone, maybe just the guy who told me once, *You're beautiful.* With someone I had my dance.

It's the senior class prom. They decorate the gym with blue balloons, sprinkle sawdust on the floor so you can shuffle around as you feel each other up as much as you can. He grips one hand and the other around the waist, and we do the two-step, nothing fancy, just a way to be close, entwined. And then the music stops and we drift apart, having nothing to say to each other, but just the joy of the dance.

That's all. ■

www.ingramcontent.com/pod-product-compliance
Lightning Source LLC
Chambersburg PA
CBHW061356140726
47997CB00003B/1226